HUgs

To

Moni

oN her 3rd

Birthday

♡

UGNAJ

2007

For Muff and Ruth,
and Gramps and Chuffs — P.K.

For Lily and Jess — S.P.

Hugs

A special bedtime prayer

by Pennie Kidd

Illustrations by
Susie Poole

 WARNER *Faith*

Hugs in the morning
When the sun begins to shine,

Hugs in the evening
when it's nearly suppertime.

Hugs in the daytime
When we go out for a walk,

Hugs in the nighttime
When I always want to talk!

Hugs when it's time to go
And I turn to wave good-bye,

Hugs when I hurt myself
And rub my eyes and cry.

Hugs when it's playtime
And my friends make me laugh,

Hugs when it's bedtime
And I must take my bath.

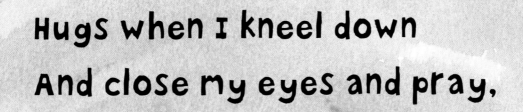

Hugs when I kneel down
And close my eyes and pray,

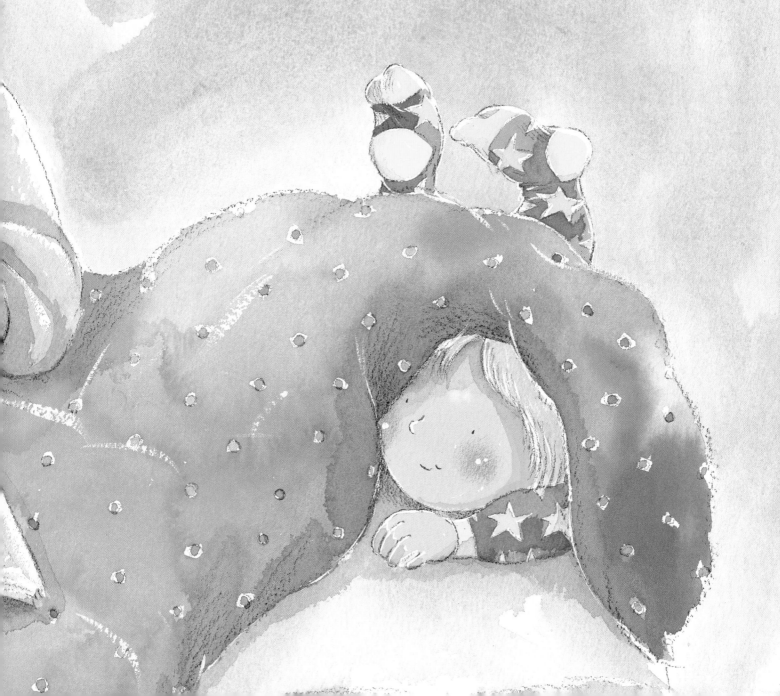

Hugs when I kiss good night
Then talk to God and say...

Thank you, God, for everyone
I meet throughout the day.

Thank you for the smiles and hugs
And love that come my way.

I'm glad I know that I am loved
Especially by you.

Help me always give a hug
And show that I love too.